THE SECRET EXPLORERS
AND THE SUNKEN TREASURE

CONTENTS

Chapter One
TIDE POOL TO ROLL CALL

Connor held his breath and tried to keep still as he watched the monsters in front of his eyes. Beasts with snappy claws hid among the rocks as jelly blobs waved their tentacled arms, and red, star-shaped creatures traveled on sticky feet. Connor wasn't scared though. In fact, he was far from it. He was in his element, face down in a tide pool. If he had gills he'd have stayed there all day! He planned to spend his whole vacation learning about California's sea life.

Eventually, he came up for air, and heard his mom calling him from the beach. She was getting a picnic lunch out of the cooler. Time to eat!

As Connor gathered his net and bucket, something caught his eye—a tiny animal trapped in the seaweed. He removed it carefully and lay it on his palm. It wasn't a creature at all, but a small plastic figure with an eye patch and a beard, like an old pirate.

How strange!

Connor never liked to remove things from the beach, but this definitely didn't belong there! He clutched it in his fist and scrambled over the rocks to join his mom.

"Look what I found!"

"Don't tell me," his mother said, passing him a sandwich. "A shell? An interesting rock? A dead crab?"

"No!" Connor laughed. "This."

He passed her the toy character, and she turned it over in her hand.

"Ah, this could have come from the cargo ship accident," his mother said. "The ship was carrying boxes of toys when it hit bad weather. It tipped to one side and several boxes fell into the ocean. It was years ago, but to this day the toys are still washing up on the shore.

Hunting them has become quite a hobby."

"Is this one of the toys from that ship?"

"It could be. It's fun to think so, isn't it?"

Connor nodded and smiled, but inside he was worried by the story. Plastic takes 450 years to decompose and it is a real danger to animals in the ocean. He looked back at the tide pools, wondering if more toys had washed up there, and that's when he saw a bright silvery flash. What was it?

Was it a fish out of water?

"I'll be back in a minute, mom!"

Connor gulped his sandwich and ran.

But it wasn't a fish. It was a small glowing disk, marked with compass points—North, East, South, and West. This could only mean one thing!

"Yes!" Connor cheered.

At the same time, a wall of sea spray washed over the rocks in front of him and hung there in the air, glistening like a crystal curtain. Connor wondered if he should tell his mom, but then he remembered—when he was called to explore, time stood still. She wouldn't miss him for a second!

As he walked into the tingling spray, there was a zap, and a flash of bright light. When it faded, Connor opened his eyes and blinked. The sticky Californian heat was gone, along with the beach and the tide pools. He was now in a cool room, humming with computers and screens.

"The Exploration Station!" he exclaimed. "Am I glad to see you!"

The walls were lined with glass cases displaying expedition treasures, such as larva rock and meteorites, ancient quills and cockle shells, and insect husks and dinosaur eggs. On the domed ceiling was a picture of the Milky Way and on the floor was a giant map of the world. This was the headquarters of the Secret Explorers, chosen for their knowledge, curiosity, and teamwork. There were eight of them in total, and it looked as if Connor, the Oceans Explorer, was the first to arrive.

"Here!" Connor called, starting the roll call.

"Here!" Roshni, the Astronomy Explorer appeared in a puff of cosmic cloud.

"Here!" said Ollie, arriving with a large purple flower in his red hair, which wasn't unusual for the Rainforest Explorer!

"Here!" said Leah. The Biology Explorer quickly inspected Ollie's flower for bugs.

"Here!"

"Here!"

Cheng, the Geology Explorer, and Gustav, the History Explorer, arrived together. Cheng's dark hair was covered in limestone dust, and Gustav brushed it carefully with his archaeology brush.

"Here!" said Kiki. The Engineering Expert had a pencil tucked behind her ear. "What's going on?"

"We won't know until we're all here," said Connor. "Where is Tamiko?"

"Here!" The Dinosaur Explorer skidded through her portal as if she was being chased

by Velociraptors. "Am I late?"

"Yes, but you had farther to come," Gustav giggled. "All the way from the Jurassic period!"

There was always laughter when they met up, but there was also always work to do. A red dot began flashing on the map. The location of the next mission!

"I know where that is," Leah said. "It's off the coast of Cornwall, in England. I've been there on vacation."

Just then, the HQ transmission screen blinked on, showing a shark with a gaping mouth. It looked as big as a bus!

"Scary!" said Ollie, with a shiver.

"You should see a T. rex," laughed Tamiko.

"It's a basking shark," Connor said.

"They're totally harmless."

"There's something in its mouth," said Kiki. "I can't figure out what it is."

The picture on the screen rotated, showing the basking shark from a different angle.

"Oh no!" Connor cried. "It's a fishing net. That shark is in trouble. I think this could be our mission." His badge lit up. "Yes! I've been chosen for the mission!"

"Good job, Connor!"

The explorers looked at each other excitedly. For every mission, two explorers were selected to go into the field. Who else would it be?

"It's me!" Kiki's hand shot up in surprise, and she pointed to her glowing badge. "That's a little strange! Why would rescuing a shark need an engineering expert?" Leah shrugged. "The Exploration Station never gets it wrong."

"Time to get the transport!" Roshni sang, pressing a large button on the wall.

A hatch in the floor slid open, and a rusty old go-kart rose from its underground garage. This was The Beagle, named after the ship of the great naturalist, Charles Darwin. It could tackle any terrain and survive every temperature, and it had been all around the world—sky high and ocean deep.

Kiki and Connor settled into the battered seats and both gave thumbs up. Cheng, Gustav, Leah, Ollie, Tamiko and Roshni sat at their computers.

"Ready?" Connor asked.

Kiki nodded. "Ready!"

She pressed the GO button on the dashboard. The go-kart rumbled and then they were enveloped in a blinding light. The Beagle clattered and groaned, and there was a loud clunk as its wheels folded away.

"It's transforming!" Connor said.

"Into what?" Kiki asked.

"I guess we'll find out!"

Almost as quickly as it had started, The Beagle's shuddering came to a sudden stop. Around them, the light had mellowed to soft sunshine, and a pale blue sky stretched overhead. Kiki looked down.

"The Beagle's a boat," she gasped. "And it looks like we're the crew!"

"Although—look! We're not alone," Connor pointed at the shoreline, where a huge ship was tucked between the rocks. A telescope rolled out from under his seat and Connor quickly put it to his eye.

He saw that the ship had rickety decks, rigging ropes, and a crow's nest. At the top, there was a black flag, which was marked with a skull and crossbones.

"What do you see?" Kiki asked excitedly.

Connor gulped. "Pirates!"

Chapter Two
A PIRATE'S LIFE

The tide began to wash Connor and Kiki toward the cove and closer to the big ship. It had arched hulls, yellowed sails, barrels, and ropes. Had they gone back in time?

"I'm not sure I actually want to meet a pirate," Kiki said.

"Me either," Connor remembered the snarl on the plastic toy's face. "But I don't think we have much choice!"

As they got closer, Connor spotted the ship's crew—there were a few on board, but most of them were on the small sandy beach. He raised his telescope again. They weren't fighting or swigging rum. Instead, some appeared to be building sandcastles and digging moats, and others were eating sandwiches out of little lunch boxes!

"I don't think we need to worry about them," Connor said, feeling quite relieved. "It looks like a group of vacationers. Maybe they can even help us. If they've been sailing around on that big boat, someone may have seen the shark. Let's ask!"

"Great idea," Kiki said. She yanked an engine cord and the little boat began purring. She dusted her hands. "I've got the motor working, so we'll be there in no time!"

Connor and Kiki chugged slowly into the cove. When they were close to the beach, they leapt out, squealing at the freezing water against their shins as they tied the mooring rope around a large rock.

"Ahoy there!" said a woman, striding toward them. She had a short brown bob and a canvas shoulder bag. She didn't look like an olden days pirate.

She didn't look like an olden days anything!

"Ahoy!" Kiki waved. "I hope we're not interrupting your lunch."

"Not at all! My name is Caroline Flush, and I'm the leader of the Craggy Cove Archaeology Society. We're just doing a little digging."

"Oh, we thought you were making sand castles," Kiki said with a giggle.

"We sometimes do that as well," Caroline smiled. "But only when the more serious digging is done."

"What exactly are you digging for?" Connor asked.

"We're looking for evidence," Caroline raised her eyebrows at them. "Three hundred years ago this place was riddled with smugglers and pirates. The cove is of

particular interest, because it has two headlands, which means that any ship moored here is invisible, unless you're looking at the beach head on."

Connor and Kiki gazed up at the towering cliffs that were all around them. Craggy Cove looked like it was a bite taken out of the land.

"It's sheltered from storms, too," Kiki said. She could see how the headlands would break up any big waves from the left or right.

"And sheltered from the eyes of the law!" Caroline said with a wink. "Some even think that Blackbeard came to this very cove to unload his stolen treasure."

"THE Blackbeard?" Kiki gasped. "The one who gathered a pirate army?"

"The one who put smoking candles in his beard?" Connor added.

"Yes, that notorious brute quite possibly used the cove to smuggle contraband. They've been filled in now, but there used to be tunnels that led deep into the ground, with exits to the surface in some hidden spot, perfect for smuggling."

"Are you looking for Blackbeard, then?" Connor asked.

"No, we're interested in another pirate—a local villain named Briggs

Lockhart. He was known for his long red ringlets, his fine clothing and his ruthless search for treasure. Rumor has it, his ship, *The Swashbuckle*, was smashed against the coast. Come and see what we've found."

Caroline led the way to a trestle table, where digging tools were laid alongside boxes of pottery shards and metal scraps.

"Is that an ancient coin?" Kiki asked.

"Why is there a marble in this bottle?" Connor asked at the same time.

"To stop the liquid sloshing out," Caroline explained. "We think all of these things came from *The Swashbuckle*."

"What about the boat itself?" Kiki asked. She pointed to the pirate ship. "Is that it over there? Did you put it back together?"

Caroline laughed. "No, no. *The Swashbuckle* hasn't been found yet. That one is owned by the Craggy Cove Archaeology Society—you can only reach the cove by boat."

"But why do you have the pirate flag flying?" Kiki asked. "It looks a bit scary!"

"I suppose it does a bit. But it's for a good reason. You see, back in the olden days, a rival flag would have caused enemy pirate ships to fight. We're hoping that our Jolly Roger flag might lure *The Swashbuckle* to us. It's just our bit of fun."

"What's *The Swashbuckle's* flag?"

"A black flag with a white octopus on it, holding a cutlass in each arm."

"Creepy!" Kiki said.

"Octopuses aren't creepy!" Connor protested. "They're related to snails. Although they are much more intelligent. Speaking of sea creatures, is there any chance you may have seen a basking shark in these waters?"

"I'll ask the diggers." Caroline gave a toot on a whistle she wore around her neck, and her crew hurried toward the discoveries table. "No new findings, but these children would like to know if any of you spotted a basking shark near here."

"I did notice a dark shape in the water when we sailed in. Just over there," a young man pointed beyond the headland. "I thought it was a shoal of fish, but come to think of it, it did have a sharky shape. Although I'm sure it was too big to be a shark!"

"Thank you," Connor said. "That sounds like it. Basking sharks are enormous!"

"And good luck with *The Swashbuckle*," Kiki shouted, as they ran toward The Beagle. "I just know that it's going to turn up for a fight!"

On board, Kiki yanked the motor cord,

and the boat began to chug again.
They sailed carefully around the cove's rocks
and into the open sea, searching for dark
shapes as they glided through the water.

"I can't see anything," Kiki sighed.

Connor stood up abruptly. "I can see something!" He pointed. "Or perhaps that should be 'some fin.'. Look Kiki, over there..."

Chapter Three
SHARK SEARCH

Kiki couldn't tell where Connor was pointing, but before she could ask, the thing with a fin leapt out of the water, and high into the air.

"It's a dolphin!" Kiki cried.

"Lots of them," said Connor. "There must be at least twenty."

The pod of dolphins skittered along the side of The Beagle, leaping high, and diving back down in beautiful arcs, sewing paths through the waves, and chatting with clicks and whistles. They were so playful that their joy was infectious, and Connor and Kiki found themselves laughing and cheering along with their new friends. That was until one large dolphin leapt up and landed in the water with such force, that it sent a huge wave over the side of the boat!

Connor shook himself. "I think that was a wake-up call to get back to work."

Kiki nodded. "If the shark isn't going to just appear, perhaps we can see if The Beagle has anything that will help us find it."

"The Beagle always has what we need," Connor agreed.

They pulled the storage boxes from under the seats and flipped open the lids and compartments. Apart from the usual safety items like flares and life jackets, they found scuba diving gear, which included masks, flippers, and air tanks.

"Ooh, look!" Kiki said, holding a small hexagonal machine, with a glass dome and propellors. "I think it's an underwater drone. I've been building a sky drone at home, but this is something else!"

"Amazing," Connor breathed.

"I know! There's nothing more satisfying than designing a gadget and getting all the little parts working perfectly."

"No... I mean that!" Connor said, pointing to the giant shape gliding beneath their boat. "That's it. That's the shark!"

"It's enormous!" Kiki's eyes widened.

"They can grow up to 40 feet long, and weigh as much as a double-decker bus. This one is definitely at the larger end of the scale."

"And they're harmless?" Kiki asked, nervously. "How sure are you about that?"

Connor chuckled. "Basking sharks only eat zooplankton, which are teeny tiny sea creatures that float near the surface. That's how basking sharks got their name, since they are often found near the surface too, basking in the sunshine!"

"It's not basking now," Kiki said.

Instead, the shark was heading downward, getting deeper into the ocean.

"We'd better follow it. We need to free it from that netting," Connor said.

Kiki handed Connor some scuba diving gear from the storage. They clambered into the wetsuits and adjusted their masks, sitting side by side on the edge of The Beagle.

"Ready, set . . ."

"Go!" Connor said, falling backward into the water. Kiki splashed down next to him.

When the froth had cleared and the water had settled, they looked around. Under the water, Connor marveled at the otherworldliness of the ocean. It was here on Earth, but it looked like a totally different planet. Huge shoals of fish, with blank eyes and pouty mouths, sailed past them, and bubbles rose from the deep in wavy strings. It wasn't an environment Kiki was all that familiar with and Connor knew that, so he clapped his hands to get her attention and nodded, asking her if she was okay.

She nodded back, yes.

They swam deeper, and the water was so clear, that they soon spotted the basking shark. Connor pushed his palms downward, gesturing to go slowly. They didn't want to scare it. But as they got nearer, they could see it was already in distress. It was jerking its head, trying to free itself from the fishing net, which was trailing from its mouth, the end of it trapped inside the shark's gills.

Kiki clapped and raised her hands and shoulders in a question: *what shall we do?*

Connor pointed upward and they swam to the surface, so that they could remove their mouthpieces and talk.

"It won't survive if we don't help it," Connor said. "Its gills are important, not only for getting oxygen from the water, but also for catching the zooplankton. If they don't work properly, they can drown, or possibly starve."

"Poor thing!" Kiki cried. "But how are we going to free it? I'm pretty nervous about getting close to something so big."

"And it'll be scared of us, too,"

Connor said, blinking salt water from his eyes. "If we startle it, it might swim away and we'd never be able to help. We need to think of something fast, because if we don't, we'll fail our mission!"

Chapter Four
THE UNDERWATER WORLD

Full of determination, Connor and Kiki went back under the water to find the shark. They found it a few yards along, swimming slowly toward the headland rocks. It was near the surface again with its mouth as wide open as it could manage. It was an incredible sight—a huge, beautiful shark in its natural environment, with the sun above

illuminating its enormous silhouette, and an underwater forest below. Because they were so near the headland, the waters were shallower, and it was easy to see the bottom. Anemones with green and pink tentacles stuck themselves to rocky boulders, so they could snatch proteins in the water.

Connor clapped at Kiki for her attention and pointed at the marine life around them. He wanted her to see why he was so passionate about the oceans. He showed her a cluster of jewel anemones, their little green cups decorated with purple gemlike blobs; a group of whiskery, bristly gurnards; and a huge white jellyfish with trailing tentacles and a purple crisscross pattern on its dome. Connor made a cross sign with his fingers. These were compass jellyfish and they could sting. Kiki nodded that she understood, and then backed away.

Then, from nowhere, a huge shoal of mackerel appeared. Their backs were striped with blue, black, and green, and they had an oily rainbow sheen, which sparkled through the surface of the water in the sunshine. Connor noticed how Kiki was looking in awe at everything, and he was relieved to see that she was enjoying the mission, too. Although, they still hadn't figured out why she had been chosen. It was definitely something to do with the shark, but... Where was the shark?

The mackerel shoal had disappeared, and they realized that the shark had too. Oh no! They looked around them frantically, but there was no sign of the basking shark. Connor motioned for them to go up.

They met at The Beagle and when Connor took his mask off, he was upset. "I knew I shouldn't have stared at those fish for long!" He noticed that Kiki was smiling. "Why are you smiling? Do you know something I don't? Haven't we just failed the mission?"

"Not yet. Beagle to the rescue!" Kiki said.

She heaved herself on board.
"We still have the drone, remember?"

Back on board, Connor watched, impressed, as Kiki plunged the drone into the sea and immediately got to grips with the steering, practicing by driving it all the way around the boat and back again. Then, she sent it away from The Beagle and into the depths of the sea. They looked at the screen as the drone propelled its way through the rocks and around the headland.

"That's awesome, Kiki," Connor said. "We're bound to spot the shark with this."

"Of course we will. Look, there's the mackerel shoal heading out to sea... Nothing there... nothing there... Oh! The drone's stuck! It looks like it's caught on a huge clump of kelp."

"Let's go. If we lose more time, the shark will be even farther away," Connor said.

Kiki pulled the motor cord and The Beagle chugged to the place the drone had gotten stuck. They didn't need to look for long. The kelp patch was huge, the top floating on the surface like a pool inflatable.

"What's that smell?" Kiki asked, as they neared. "Oh look, there it is!" She leaned out over the kelp float and plunged her hand

into the mush to fish out the drone. "Urgh, that's not good."

She showed Connor the gunge that was jammed in the drone's propellers. The stench of old fish was overpowering. And so was the feeling that after everything, they had truly failed the mission. Connor sighed. The ocean was his subject. How could he have been so careless as to lose a giant shark?

"Hey, Connor," Kiki said, as she patted his shoulder reassuringly. "Don't give up—it's not over yet. We just need a little help from our friends!"

Chapter Five
THE DREAM TEAM

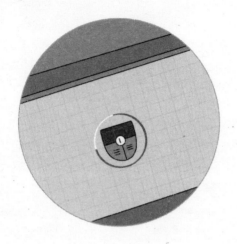

"Exploration Station, do you read me?" Kiki waited a second and then repeated: "Exploration Station, do you read me?"

There was a crackle and a fizz as The Beagle's dashboard screen came to life.

"Loud and clear, Kiki!" said Cheng.

The other faces then appeared too. Gustavo, Tamiko, Leah, Ollie, and Roshni.

They all waved and Connor felt his worries subside. It was so good to see them!

"How's the mission going?" asked Roshni.

"Did you see the shark? Tell us about its teeth!" Tamiko said excitedly.

"Badly; yes; and basking sharks have lots of tiny teeth—in that order," Connor replied.

"How can it be going badly if you've found the shark?" Leah said, concerned.

"We lost it. We got distracted and . . ."

"He's blaming himself," Kiki said. "In fact, we got separated by a giant shoal of fish. When it cleared, the shark had gone. We just need some help to find it."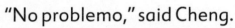

"No problemo," said Cheng. He fiddled with the computer controls and The Beagle's screen divided into two—one side showing the gang, and the other side displayed a map of the seabed, marked with all of its rocks and trenches, as well as the direction of the current.

"If the current is going south, then that's where the plankton would have floated," said Ollie. "A bit like seeds in the wind."

"And the shark probably followed," added Leah. "Although not too close to the shore because there are huge rock formations there."

"Those rock formations are beautiful though," added Cheng.

"Throughout history, those rocks have been a pain in the bottom..."

"Gustavo!" the team gasped, including Connor and Kiki.

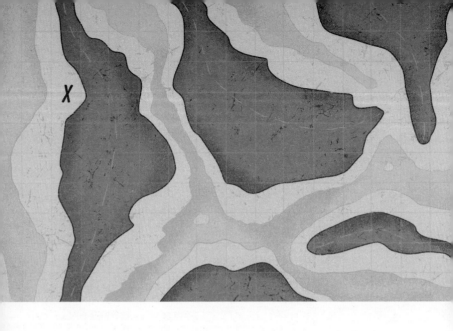

"Let me finish!" he said with a chuckle. "A pain in the bottom... *of boats*. The sea around the Cornish coast is littered with shipwrecks."

"And I bet the pirates waited until one was in trouble so they could attack," Kiki said.

"Like the naughty Briggs Lockhart," Connor said.

Huh? All the faces at the Exploration Station looked confused.

"Oh nothing," Kiki laughed.

"As I was saying," Gustavo coughed. "You need to be very careful. Some of those underwater rocks come so close to the surface that you could easily strand the poor Beagle."

"And it's battered enough!" said Roshni.

The Beagle's dashboard bleeped and blooped as if it was agreeing, and everyone laughed.

"Okay, thanks team. We'd better try and get back on track!" Connor said.

"See you later, alligator!" said Leah.

Connor and Kiki didn't waste time. Following the route they'd planned out on their map, with an X marked in the spot they thought the shark might be, they headed out to sea. But within minutes, they felt The Beagle straining to keep on course.

It was if a magnetic force was attempting to tug them away.

"It's a current!" Kiki said, pointing to a line on the map. "A big one. I don't think we can fight it."

"Then let's go with it. The shark was probably pulled by it too, so we're more likely to be going the right way."

With her hands resting loosely on the steering lever, Kiki allowed The Beagle to be directed by the water, and the little boat whistled and beeped as if it was enjoying the break.

"Whoah, steer around this part!" Connor said hurriedly, noticing a cluster of rocks.

Kiki kicked The Beagle into gear and wrestled the boat into safer waters. Suddenly, the current dissolved, and they found themselves in much calmer water. Connor pointed to the X. They were close.

"Let's turn off the engine, so we don't scare it," he suggested. "Oh wow! There's a coral reef just over there!" He sighed dreamily. Cold-water corals were fascinating, and so were the animals that lived in the reef structure. Connor thought about how much he would love to explore.

"Ahem," Kiki coughed. "Aren't we supposed to be looking for the shark?"

"Absolutely," Connor said. "I am looking... and there it is!"

A large rubbery back slid through the water ahead of them.

Kiki spoke into the microphone on the dashboard, and hoped that her voice would carry back to the Exploration Station. "X marks the spot! Good job, Explorers!"

But, now that they'd found it, how were they going to save it?

Chapter Six
TRAPPED IN A NET

Connor paced the small deck of The Beagle, scratching his head.

"Why don't you start by telling me what you know about basking sharks," Kiki suggested. "Sometimes, when there's a problem with one of my machines, I take it apart and check all the pieces. If you break the situation down into small parts, the answer might be found in the tiniest detail."

"Yes, good plan!" Connor agreed. "Basking sharks are the second biggest fish in the sea."

"You mean there's one bigger than that?"

"Yes, a whale shark."

"Oh wow!" Kiki said, shaking her head in disbelief.

"Whale sharks are also harmless," Connor added. "So, the basking shark is the second biggest fish in the sea...

and they live for around fifty years."

"And we're going to make sure this one does, too," Kiki said.

Connor smiled at her. "Oh, and they rarely swim alone," he remembered. "So this is actually quite unusual."

"It must have gotten separated from its friends when it tried to shake off the net!"

"Yes. But since they have a very strong sense of smell, they will hopefully find one another again."

"They can sniff each other out in this huge ocean?"

"I'm not certain. But I know they use smell to find food, and this one is really hungry . . ."

"Why have you stopped talking? What is it?" Kiki asked.

"I think I have an idea!"

"A smelly one?"

"Yes! We could distract it with the smell of food, and while it's busy sniffing, we can get close to it and cut away the netting."

"Great! Although, how do we get enough zooplankton together to create a really big stink?" Kiki asked with a shrug. "We can't even see zooplankton!"

A really big stink... Connor's eyes lit up. "I know. The rotting kelp patch had a strong smell. It must have been the gunk inside it. If we get some kelp and crush it to release a scent, maybe it'll attract the shark."

"Do you think it could work?" Kiki asked, not waiting for the answer before she trailed her hand in the water by the boat, tugging at kelp ribbons.

Connor quickly slipped overboard and swam to where there was more kelp, pulling the bobbly, rubbery strands to the surface, so that Kiki could pull them up onto the deck of The Beagle. She bent and snapped each ribbon and passed it back to Connor, who made a bundle of the broken seaweed in his arms. When he could carry no more, he set off toward the shark.

"Connor!" Kiki cried. "The shark has turned around and is coming toward you!"

Connor ducked his head and looked through his mask. He saw the giant shape cruising his way. Despite knowing that the beast was harmless, he still felt his skin prickle with nerves. It was so big and he was so small! He swam to the surface.

"Mash some more, Kiki!"

"Alright!"

Together, they collected and mashed as much as they could, until they had a giant ball of kelp, floating just a couple of yards away from the boat. The shark was getting closer and closer, drawn in by the kelp smell. It was working! It began to nudge and nuzzle at the kelp, as it floated alongside it. It seemed transfixed. It was now or never!

Connor gulped as he looked at the giant mouth in front of him, wondering if he could somehow be sucked into the belly of the beast. It was one thing being interested in giants of the sea, but another thing altogether to see them this close up!

It's harmless, he told himself. *Completely harmless!* And if I don't help it, no one will.

Determined, he swam toward the shark, steering clear of its gaping jaws. He stopped alongside it, out of its eyeline, and trailed his hand along the rough rubber of its skin. His fear began to disappear and give way to wonder. He was in the ocean with the second biggest fish in the world! Feeling braver, he swam back up the body and round to the mouth. He peered inside, and could see exactly where the net was caught. It was wrapped around the shark's snout!

Connor pushed the net off its nose and then gently tugged it, to free it from the gills inside. But the fish net wasn't budging—not from that position. Connor gulped.

Pulling himself along the netting and holding tight in case a rush of water pushed him too deep inside the cavernous mouth, Connor changed his position so that he was facing the mouth and his head was now inside the wide entrance. He tugged again. The shark shook a little, disturbed by the discomfort. But above them, another pile of kelp landed with a splat—Kiki was doing her best, and the shark pushed forward to investigate. With the shark's forward movement, Connor was now even deeper inside the gullet, but he used the awkward situation and the momentary slack in the netting to his advantage. He quickly flicked the mesh so that it unhooked itself from where it was caught. Connor gave one last almighty pull...

He backed away quickly, dragging the netting free. The basking shark thrashed again and Connor didn't wait to see what would happen next—everything was telling him to get back on the boat. He climbed aboard, reeling the net in after him, and rolling it into a tight ball. That would be going in the trash on land, so that it never hurt another marine creature ever again!

He looked back at the shark, but it was no longer at the surface.

"You did it!" Kiki cheered. "Let's go under and watch it swim away."

Connor nodded. "Alright! Seeing as I'm already wet." They laughed.

Back in the water, they looked at the area beneath the surface, but the giant was nowhere to be seen. Kiki clapped her hands and pointed downward. Something was causing a sandstorm on the seabed. It was the shark!

Connor brought his hands to his face. What had he done? Had he hurt it? Was it wounded?

Kiki tugged his arm and then drew a smile across her face with her finger. It was happy! Happy to be free! Connor looked again. The shark wasn't writhing, it was rolling! He drew his hand over his forehead, in a gesture of *phew!* and both of them looked back at the grateful creature. Although, now it looked like there was something else at the bottom of the sea. The shark's rolling had stirred up the sand to reveal a structure. A coral reef! Connor would get to investigate one after all!

Kiki tapped his shoulder, and punched the water in front of her in a swooping, swashbuckling gesture. Confused, Connor looked again. And then he saw it. It wasn't a coral reef...

It was a shipwreck!

Chapter Seven
THE LOST SHIP

The two Secret Explorers looked at each other through their masks and shook their heads in amazement. What an incredible sight!

They couldn't wait to explore, but before they did, they needed to make sure the basking shark had fully recovered. The health of that beautiful creature was the most important thing. Their enormous friend had left the seabed and was now heading for the surface, ready to guzzle tons of zooplankton. Its mouth opened wider and wider; it looked like a floating underwater tunnel! Connor could hardly believe that only a few minutes ago, he'd been inside that huge gullet! He couldn't wait to tell the others that he'd been in the mouth of a shark! When the shark was back at the top, basking once again in the sunshine, Connor gave Kiki a big thumbs up. Thanks to brains and bravery, and The Beagle of course, the mission had been a success.

But there was no way they were going to go home before they'd investigated the shipwreck! Without even waiting for each other to give the signal to go, they both powered down, headfirst through the water, with a stream of bubbles flying from their flippers. Just above the site, they stopped and looked down, treading water.

Beneath them, the sunken ship was almost upright, only leaning slightly to one side where it had settled on the seabed. It was still recognizable as an old-fashioned sailing ship. Its gunwale was intact, as were the vast arching wooden strakes, which were like the ribs of the ship, holding the planks in place. Most of the original wood was still attached to the beams, although a few areas had softened and rotted away. Fish darted in and out of the holes as if they were playing a game of tag. The whole structure was covered in barnacles and anemones. Crabs scuttled, and sea snails oozed all over. It might once have sailed the high seas, but this boat was now a home to thousands of marine creatures. But who did it belong to before it became the property of the fat-lipped fish and limpets?

Connor swam over the top of the deck, looking for a way to get in. *Imagine if we found something historical inside*, he thought. *Or even an artifact to take back to the Exploration Station!* But the only safe way in was through the hatch in the hull, and it was blocked by the mast, which had snapped and fallen across it. Connor shrugged at his teammate—what do we do now? Kiki tapped her head. She had an idea!

She swam away and quickly returned with a long lump of wood that she had found on the upper deck. Connor frowned—how was adding more wood going to help? But then, as Kiki wedged the wood under the mast and began to push down on the opposite end of it, he realized what she was doing. The wooden log was acting as a lever, of course! Kiki was the engineering expert, and she knew exactly what she was doing! With a loud creak, the mast lifted and hung, suspended in the water. Before it could drift downward again, Connor pushed it away from the hatch.

Now there was nothing lying in the way of a good exploration!

Kiki and Connor high-fived and looked down into the hole. It was bustling with life! Protected from strong currents by the walls, the seaweed and plants inside the hull grew thick and lush. Mussels created a bristly coating and great clouds of fish busied themselves eating the nutrients. Eels slid in and out of nooks, and huge crabs feasted on scraps.

The ship had become a manmade reef! It reminded Connor of a show he'd seen about New York subway cars that had been dropped into the Atlantic to create underwater habitats. When it came to the oceans, humans could do some really good things. It was the things they did without thinking that did the damage— dumping litter, dredging the seafloor, and dropping a cargo full of plastic toys!

CLICK CLICK!

Kiki was clapping, trying to get his attention, and Connor realized he'd been lost in thought.

She pointed down. *Let's go!*

Careful not to upset the incredible marine ecosystem, they swam into the darkness. As their eyes adjusted to the low light, they spotted even more creatures:

urchins, sponges, and sea anemones. Kiki made a high-pitched squeal and Connor turned to see her pointing frantically at a large bluish creature. It had a long body, a crablike shell, a fanned tail, and giant claws. A lobster. And what a big one! But if Kiki thought that was weird and wonderful, what would she make of a spider crab? Connor pointed out the huge beast with the orange spiky shell the size of a dinner plate. It was edging out of a dark hole.

But when he looked more closely, Connor saw that the hole was the mouth of a cylinder. An oil drum perhaps? He swept aside some seaweed, and then he saw it. A cannon!

He turned to show Kiki, but she had already found another one. There were lots of cannons, and the boulders, which they had thought were rocks, were actually cannonballs. Connor pushed his fist down, and then up again in a swinging gesture, mouthing 'Arrrr.' A pirate ship! Kiki nodded. Then she motioned around and around with her hand. Let's keep looking!

They swept the sand away from the canons, looking for inscriptions or dates. As they did so, they began to spot glints of metal, caught in the shells and stones. Kiki rushed to pick one up, rubbing

it on her wetsuit to remove the dirt and make it shine. She held it up to the sunlight that filtered through the hatch above them. It was round, the color of dull gold. It was a coin. An ancient gold coin!

There must have been hundreds! Connor began to gather a pile of them and beckoned Kiki to help, but his friend had now gone to investigate something else.

Kiki had seen strange markings on the floor. They didn't look like scratches or damage, since the lines were too deep and smooth. It was as if they'd been etched by a branding tool. Was it a picture of some sort? She pulled Connor's arm and motioned for him to help. Together they edged the sand farther and farther back, revealing an image that had been carved into the wooden planks. Some of the grooves were filled with sand and debris, and they used shells to dig them out. When they had been through every line and loop, they swam up to the roof of the hull so they could see the whole picture. A few lines had eroded over time, but what they saw was unmistakeable.

An octopus. And in each leg, a cutlass. This was *The Swashbuckle!* They'd found it!

Chapter Eight

PRECIOUS TREASURE

Connor and Kiki swam back to The Beagle as quickly as they could. They pulled themselves on board, gasping with exhaustion and exhilaration. Noting the exact spot with an X on The Beagle's mapping screen, they chugged back toward Craggy Cove. They couldn't wait to share the good news.

On shore, the little group was busy
measuring out the beach, and searching
the rocks for signs of a centuries-old
shipping disaster. The head archaeologist,
Caroline Flush, was standing with her
pants rolled up and her feet in the
shallows, gazing at the ocean and enjoying
a cheese sandwich.

"Ahoy!" she said, spotting them. She
waved her sandwich in the air.

"Ahoy there!" said Kiki and Connor.

As they neared, Caroline held her sandwich in her teeth and used her hands to grab the mooring rope. She tugged The Beagle toward the beach until it was safely wedged in the sand.

"Did you find your shark?" she asked, her eyes sparkling.

"We did," Kiki said. "We found it and we saved it!"

"It had netting stuck in its gills," Connor said.

"How on earth did you untangle it?"

"I had to swim in its mouth!" Connor said.

Caroline crossed her arms in disbelief. "Well I never. You two really are a couple of adventurers!"

"We're explorers actually," Kiki said. She looked at Connor and nodded.

Connor nodded back. "And we found something you might be interested in."

Caroline blew her whistle with an almighty toot and the Craggy Cove archaeologists tiptoed as quickly as they could though their measured-out areas of beach, and their piles of rock and pottery fragments.

"What is it?" panted Willoughby, an elderly man with a white wispy beard. "Is there a lead?"

"I just unearthed a buckle," said a young girl, holding up her find.

"Un-sanded, you mean!" said another.

"Oh, we have something even more exciting than that to share with you." Caroline put a hand on the shoulders of the child either side of her. "We have *The Swashbuckle*."

"What do you mean?" asked a woman in jeans, with sand in her eyelashes.

"We mean the ship. We found the ship,"

said Kiki, laughing as she watched a gaggle of mouths drop open.

"It's just out there beyond the headland," Connor said. "We marked the exact location."

"Impossible! We've been searching for it for months." The old man tutted.

Kiki sprinkled a handful of the gold coins on the sand and the archaeologists swooped on them, picking them up

and turning them over in the light to read their inscriptions. Then there was a loud chorus of delight.

"These are florins!"

*"**Real** florins!"*

"Pirate treasure!"

"Where's the wreck? Please tell us!"

Caroline smiled. "Yes, perhaps you can tell us now where it is?"

"We could..." Kiki started.

"And we will..." Connor continued. "But only if you promise us one thing..."

"Do you want your name on the discovery papers? Headlines in the paper? Free membership of the Craggy Cove Archaeology Society... with sandwiches all paid for? Anything you want. Anything!"

"We don't want fame. We don't even want the florins. All we ask is that you treat *The Swashbuckle* with care.

The ship is part of the ocean now and the ocean is part of the ship. It's become a reef —a home for thousands of creatures; a precious habitat for fish, plants, and animals."

There was a lot of murmuring, and then Caroline blew her whistle. "Listen up, Craggy Covers. No one cares about *The Swashbuckle* more than us, so it's only right that we get to know it inside and out before we report it. And when we do, I will insist that the wreck is left undisturbed as Craggy Cove's curious, historical reef."

"Yes, I suppose that does make sense,"

Willoughby said, nodding furiously.

"And we can bring out any loose pirate artifacts," said the woman in jeans.

"We could do scuba tours!" suggested a young man, who had tuna on his chin.

"Or open a museum!" said another.

While the archaeologists fell into excited chatter about all the possibilities ahead, Caroline turned to Connor and Kiki.

"*The Swashbuckle reef* will be safe with us, I promise," she said. "Now, my wonderful explorers, we'd all better be on our way before the tide goes out. Man the decks!"

Connor and Kiki pushed The Beagle off the sand and scrambled aboard, turning to take one more look at the eccentric group at Craggy Bay, who were busy cleaning, packing up their findings, and getting their ship ready with happy shouts of "Arrrr."

They floated away from the land. The coastline shrunk behind them, and ahead of them the large sun was making its way down toward the horizon, spreading a peachy glow that rippled on the water.

"Now what?" Kiki asked. "Is there a button I should be pressing on the Beagle?"

"Or maybe, it's not ready to go," Connor said. "It hasn't said all its goodbyes. Look!"

Curving toward them through the water was a large black fin and a brown shiny back. Behind it was another, and another. Three basking sharks, swimming freely!

The first one raised its snout out of the water, and Connor reached to touch it.

"Be careful out there," he whispered.

The basking shark quickly changed direction, sending a splash of water right onto Connor's face.

Kiki laughed, The Beagle beeped and then there was a sudden flash of light as the boat shuddered and shook and clunked. A mist swirled around them.

"This vehicle is such a drama queen!" Kiki laughed.

There was another flash of light, and then it was over. The Beagle was now a go-kart with sunken seats and four wheels, and their surroundings were unusually calm. There were no rocking waves or salty spray—just peace and cool air. When the mist cleared, it was like they'd never left.

"The Exploration Station!" Connor shouted happily.

The rest of the Secret Explorers spun around in their swivel chairs. "You're back!"

"Tell us more about the shark! Was it as big as a megalodon?" Tamiko quizzed.

"Basking sharks are huge, but not quite as big as a megalodon!" Kiki laughed. "Connor managed to untangle the poor creature from some fishing net. He even had to swim inside its mouth!"

"Whoah!" Tamiko exclaimed.

"Bravo, Connor!" Gustavo cried.

"But why did you go, Kiki?" Roshni asked. "What were you needed for in the end?"

"I managed to drive The Beagle when it turned into a boat," Kiki said.

"And we needed a drone to help us look for the shark. It worked exactly like the one I built at home."

"Plus without her quick thinking, we'd never have been able to explore inside that wreck."

"A wreck?" Gustavo gasped. "What sort of wreck?"

"A pirate ship. It was hundreds of years old."

"Were there any skeletons?" Leah asked, her eyes popping with excitement.

"None that we saw," Connor replied. "Just lots of seaweed—it was like a jungle in a boat."

"Nice one!" Ollie nodded approvingly.

"And there were lots of crabs, and fish, and anemones," Kiki added.

"Were there any cool rocks?" Cheng tried, feeling left out.

"Well, you might be able to tell us what this is made of," Connor said, handing him a florin.

Cheng grinned as he held it to the light. "That's gold." He handed it back. "What will you do with it?"

"It's a Secret Explorer find, so it stays right here at the Secret Explorer headquarters."

Connor slid open a glass cabinet and rested the pirate treasure on a shelf. "Mission accomplished."

"Amazing!" Roshni said. "Every time there's a mission, it just gets better!"

They high fived each other, then pushed in the chairs and sent The Beagle back down to its underground garage. When the Exploration Station was cleaned up, they turned to look at each other.

"Guess it's time to go," Leah said.

"Yep, time to go," said Roshni. "I need to get ready for stargazing later."

"I know what I'll be dreaming of tonight," Kiki sighed. "Pirates, sharks, and sailing the seas. That was a great adventure, Connor."

"A brilliant exploration, Kiki," Connor agreed. "Until next time, everyone!"

"Bye, Connor!"

Connor stepped through the glowing door. Sea spray washed over his face and he found himself back at the rock pools, baking in the Californian sun.

"That was a biggie!"

Connor turned to see his mother, tiptoeing across the rocks toward him, holding a sandwich. He smiled as he remembered Caroline Flush and the Craggy Covers.

"A big what?" he asked.

"A freak wave! For a moment I couldn't see you," she said.

"Why aren't you on the beach reading?" Connor asked.

"I thought I'd come and see what the fuss was all about. Come on, why don't you show me what's in these rock pools! Where are the creatures? I can't see any."

Connor grinned. "You have to be patient," he explained. "You brush aside the weed and then wait until your eyes adjust. When that happens, you suddenly spot things, like baby crabs, little fish, or shiny scales!"

"It's a bit like looking for treasure," his mother said.

Connor smiled. "Yes, it is. Only better!"

A HISTORY OF PIRATES

Pirates have been around since ancient times, but their height, known as The Golden Age of Piracy, was between 1690 and 1796. During this time, more than 5,000 pirates were at sea.

WHO WERE PIRATES?

Originally, pirates were sailors with great knowledge of the seas. They began to question why they should go through difficult journeys to transport goods for little pay, when they could just steal them from others on the water!

A PIRATE'S LIFE FOR ME!

FLAGS

Some pirate ships displayed flags, such as the 'Jolly Roger,' which were used to intimidate sailors and convince them to give up their goods.

TREASURE

Pirates would often steal goods such as sugar and spices. Though these might not sound as appealing as gold or jewels, they could be traded for supplies or money.

PETS

Parrots were very valuable to pirates. They were a symbol of status, and the sociable and intelligent animals could be taught tricks, keeping the pirates company on their voyages. Once home, pirates could also benefit by selling these exotic, colorful animals.

SCUBA DIVING

Since the development of scuba gear (SCUBA stands for Self Contained Underwater Breathing Apparatus), humans have become more aware of what lies beneath the sea, removing some of the mystery of the oceanic world.

Divers are now able to swim to depths of 100 ft (30 m) or more, and this has led to many discoveries, such as shipwrecks, unusual marine life, and even ancient cities.

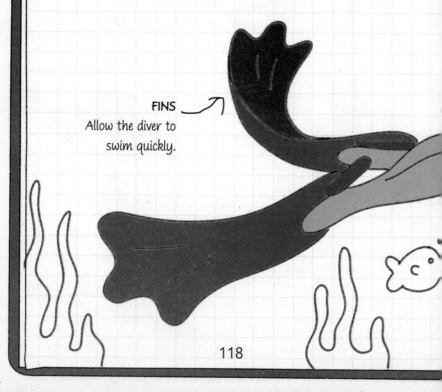

FINS
Allow the diver to swim quickly.

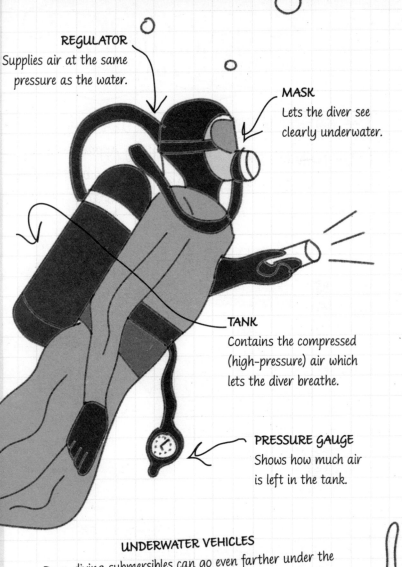

REGULATOR
Supplies air at the same pressure as the water.

MASK
Lets the diver see clearly underwater.

TANK
Contains the compressed (high-pressure) air which lets the diver breathe.

PRESSURE GAUGE
Shows how much air is left in the tank.

UNDERWATER VEHICLES

Deep-diving submersibles can go even farther under the sea, since they can handle higher water pressure than humans. Scientists use these types of vehicle to investigate the deepest sea life. Some can go as far as 19,685 ft (6,000 m) underwater.

BASKING SHARK

THE BASKING SHARK

* **LATIN NAME:**
Cetorhinus maximus

* **ANIMAL TYPE:**
Fish

* **LOCATION:**
Cold to temperate waters
around the world

* **LENGTH AND WEIGHT:**
Basking sharks grow up to 39 ft
(12 m) and weigh up to 10,000
pounds (4.5 metric tons).

* **FUN FACT:**
Basking sharks swim with their
enormous mouths open, to filter
the water for food—almost like
a giant sieve on the move!

Basking sharks can
dive to depths of
2,950 ft (900 m).

QUIZ

1   How many years does it take plastic to decompose?

2   What did Blackbeard put in his beard to make him look more scary?

3   True or false: Briggs Lockhart's pirate ship was called the *Jolly Roger*.

4   True or false: A basking shark can weigh as much as a double decker bus.

5   True or false: Basking sharks don't have any teeth.

6   Which vehicles were dropped into the Atlantic Ocean to create a habitat for underwater plants and creatures?

7   How many cutlasses was the octopus holding on the *Swashbuckle's* flag?

Check your answers on page 127

GLOSSARY

ANEMONES
Small sea animals
with many tentacles,
that look a bit
like flowers.

BRUTE
A violent person.

CARGO SHIP
Ship that
carries goods.

CAVERNOUS
Large or dark room,
a bit like a cave.

CONTRABAND
Goods that are
taken in or out of
a country illegally.

COSMIC CLOUD
Cloud of dust and
gas in space.

CUTLASS
Short sword, used
by sailors.

GULLET
Tube in the throat,
which goes from
mouth to stomach.

GUNWALE
The upper edge of the side of a boat.

GURNARD
Type of fish that lives at the bottom of the sea.

HEADLAND
Narrow land which sticks out from the coast into the sea.

HULL
Main body of a boat.

INSECT HUSKS
The outer skin shed by insects when molting.

LIMPETS
Small sea creatures with snaillike shells.

MEGALODON
An extinct species of very large shark.

MOORING
Securing a boat to a fixed structure.

NATURALIST
A person who studies the natural world.

NOTORIOUS
Famous, typically for something bad.

OTHERWORLDLY
Relating to an imaginary or spiritual world.

RUTHLESS
Determined, with no pity or compassion for others.

SHEEN
A shiny surface, usually caused by reflected light.

SLACK
Loose or not tightly held.

SMUGGLING
Illegal movement of goods.

TRANSFIXED
Become motionless, usually because of fear or interest.

Quiz answers

1. 450 years

2. Smoking candles

3. False—it was called the *Swashbuckle*

4. True

5. False – they have lots of little teeth

6. Subway cars

7. Eight

DK | Penguin Random House

For Myia and Bodhi

Text for DK by Working Partners Ltd
9 Kingsway, London WC2B 6XF
With special thanks to Lucy Courtenay

Design by Collaborate Ltd
Illustrator Ellie O'Shea & Louie O'Shea
Consultant Anita Ganeri

Acquisitions Editor James Mitchem
Editor Becca Arlington
US Senior Editor Shannon Beatty
Designer Sonny Flynn
Jacket and Sales Material Coordinator Magda Pszuk
Senior Production Editor Jenny Murray, Nikoleta Parasaki
Production Controller Ena Matagic
Publishing Director Sarah Larter

First American Edition, 2023
Published in the United States by DK Publishing
1745 Broadway, 20th Floor, New York, New York, 10019

Published in Great Britain by Dorling Kindersley Limited.

A catalog record for this book
is available from the Library of Congress

ISBN: 978-0-7440-8038-4 (paperback)
ISBN: 978-0-7440-8039-1 (hardcover)

Printed and bound in Great Britain by
Clays Ltd, Elcograf S.p.A.

For the curious

www.dk.com

MIX
Paper | Supporting
responsible forestry
FSC™ C018179

This book was made with Forest
Stewardship Council™ certified
paper—one small step in DK's
commitment to a sustainable future.
**For more information go to
www.dk.com/our-green-pledge**